SOME TALES OF
THE OCCULT
FROM
CORNWALL

BY

VARIOUS AUTHORS

British Library Cataloguing-in-Publication Data
A catalogue record for this book is available from the
British Library

CONTENTS

BRAM STOKER

Abraham 'Bram' Stoker was born in Dublin, Ireland in 1847. Stoker was a semi-invalid as a child, and was bedridden until he started school at the age of seven. However, he made a full recovery and went on to excel as an athlete at Trinity College, which he enrolled at in 1864. Stoker graduated with honours in mathematics in 1870, and was also president of the university's philosophical society.

Stoker developed an interest in theatre, and became theatre critic for the *Dublin Evening Mail* in his early twenties. It was following a favourable review he gave of an 1876 Henry Irving production of *Hamlet* that Stoker and Irving struck up a friendship. Three years later, in the same year that Stoker married Florence Balcombe (whose former suitor was Oscar Wilde), he became acting-manager and then business manager of Irving's Lyceum Theatre – a post he went on to hold for 27 years. As a result of his close friendship with Irving (the most famous actor of his day), Stoker became something of a socialite. He mingled with London's high society, meeting writers such as Sir Arthur Conan Doyle, and travelled extensively in the United States, where he spent time with both Theodore Roosevelt and Walt Whitman.

While working for Irving, Stoker began to write

novels, eventually producing a total of fifteen works of fiction. Although most met with at least mild success, Stoker is best known for his 1897 publication, *Dracula*. This work – an epistolary novel weaving hypnotism, magic, the supernatural, and other elements of Gothic fiction – went on to sell over one million copies, and has never been out of print. Today, the novel and its eponymous protagonist remain so well-known that one can actually visit the castle of Count Dracula in the Transylvanian region of Romania – despite the fact that Stoker never even went there himself.

After a series of strokes, Stoker died in London in 1912, aged 64.

THE COMING OF ABEL BEHENNA

BRAM STOKER

The little Cornish port of Pencastle was bright in the early April, when the sun had seemingly come to stay after a long and bitter winter. Boldly and blackly the rock stood out against a background of shaded blue, where the sky fading into mist met the far horizon. The sea was of true Cornish hue – sapphire, save where it became deep emerald green in the fathomless depths under the cliffs, where the seal caves opened their grim jaws. On the slopes the grass was parched and brown. The spikes of furze bushes were ashy grey, but the golden yellow of their flowers streamed along the hillside, dipping out in lines as the rock cropped up, and lessening into patches and dots till finally it died away all together where the sea winds swept round the jutting cliffs and cut short the vegetation as though with ever-working aerial shears. The whole hillside, with its body of brown and flashes of yellow, was just like a colossal yellow-hammer.

The little harbour opened from the sea between towering cliffs, and behind a lonely rock, pierced with many caves and blow-holes through which the sea in storm time sent its thunderous voice, together with a fountain of drifting spume. Hence, it wound westwards in a serpentine course, guarded at its entrance by two little curving piers to left and right. These were roughly built of dark slates placed endways and held together with great beams bound with iron bands. Thence, it flowed up the rocky bed of the stream whose winter torrents had of old cut out its way amongst the hills. This stream was deep at first, with here and there, where it widened, patches of broken rock exposed at low water, full of holes where crabs and lobsters were to be found at the ebb of the tide. From amongst the rocks rose sturdy posts, used for warping in the little coasting vessels which frequented the port. Higher up, the stream still flowed deeply, for the tide ran far inland, but always calmly for all the force of the wildest storm was broken below. Some quarter mile inland the stream was deep at high water, but at low tide there were at each side patches of the same broken rock as lower down, through the chinks of which the sweet water of the natural stream trickled and murmured after the tide had ebbed away. Here, too, rose mooring posts for the fishermen's boats. At either side of the river was a row of cottages down almost on the level of high tide. They were pretty cottages, strongly and snugly built, with trim narrow gardens in front, full of old-fashioned plants, flowering currants, coloured primroses, wallflower, and stonecrop. Over the fronts of many of them climbed clematis and wisteria. The window sides and door posts of all were as white as snow, and the little pathway to each was paved with light coloured stones. At some of the doors were tiny porches, whilst at others were rustic seats cut from tree trunks or from old barrels; in nearly every case the window ledges were filled with boxes or pots of flowers or foliage plants.

Two men lived in cottages exactly opposite each other across the stream. Two men, both young, both good-looking, both prosperous, and who had been companions and rivals from their boyhood. Abel Behenna was dark with the gypsy darkness which the Phoenician mining wanderers left in their track; Eric Sanson – which the local antiquarian said was a corruption of Sagamanson – was fair, with the ruddy hue which/marked the path of the wild Norseman. These two seemed to have singled out each other from the very beginning to work and strive together, to fight for each other and to stand back to back in all endeavours. They had now put the coping-stone on their Temple of Unity by falling in love with the same girl. Sarah Trefusis was certainly the prettiest girl in Pencastle, and there was many a young man who would gladly have tried his fortune with her, but that there were two to contend against, and each of these the strongest and most resolute man in the port – except the other. The average young man thought that this was very hard, and on account of it bore no good will to either of the three principals: whilst the average young woman who had, lest worse should befall, to put up with the grumbling of her sweetheart, and the sense of being only second best which it implied, did not either, be sure, regard Sarah with friendly eye. Thus it came, in the course of a year or so, for rustic courtship is a slow process, that the two men and woman found themselves thrown much together. They were all satisfied, so it did not matter, and Sarah, who was vain and something frivolous, took care to have her revenge on both men and women in a quiet way. When a young woman in her 'walking out' can only boast one not-quite-satisfied young man, it is no particular pleasure to her to see her escort cast sheep's eyes at a better-looking girl supported by two devoted swains.

At length there came a time which Sarah dreaded, and which she had tried to keep distant – the time when she had to make her choice between the two men. She liked them both, and, indeed, either of them might have satisfied the ideas of even a more exacting girl. But her mind was so constituted that she thought more of what she might lose, than of what she might gain; and whenever she thought she had made up her mind she became instantly assailed with doubts as to the wisdom of her choice. Always the man whom she had presumably lost became endowed afresh with a newer and more bountiful crop of advantages than had ever arisen from the possibility of his acceptance. She promised each man that on her birthday she would give him his answer, and that day, the 11th of April, had now arrived. The promises had been given singly and confidentially, but each was given to a man who was not likely to forget. Early in the morning she found both men hovering round her door. Neither had taken the other into his confidence, and each was simply seeking an early opportunity of getting his answer, and advancing his suit if necessary. Damon, as a rule, does not take Pythias with him when making a proposal; and in the heart of each man his own affairs had a claim far above any requirements of friendship. So, throughout the day, they kept seeing each other out. The position was doubtless somewhat embarrassing to Sarah, and though the satisfaction of her vanity that she should be thus adored was very pleasing, yet there were moments when she was annoyed with both men for being so persistent. Her only consolation at such moments was that she saw, through the elaborate smiles of the other girls when in passing they noticed her door thus doubly guarded, the jealousy which filled their hearts. Sarah's mother was a person of commonplace and sordid ideas, and, seeing all along the state of affairs, her one intention, persistently expressed to her daughter in the plainest words, was to so arrange matters that Sarah should get all that was possible out of both men. With this purpose she had cunningly kept herself as far as possible in the background in the matter of her daughter's wooings, and watched in silence. At first Sarah had been indignant with her for her sordid views; but, as usual, her weak nature gave way before persistence, and she had now got to the stage of acceptance. She was not surprised when her mother whispered to her in the little yard behind the house: 'Go up the hillside for a while; I want to talk to these two. They're both red-hot for ye, and now's the time to get things fixed!' Sarah began a feeble remonstrance, but her mother cut her short.

'I tell ye, girl, that my mind is made up! Both these men want ye, and only one can have ye, but before ye choose it'll be so arranged that ye'll have all that both have got! Don't argy, child! Go up the hillside, and when ye come back I'll have it fixed – I see a way quite easy!' So Sarah went up the hillside through the narrow paths between the golden furze, and Mrs Trefusis joined the two men in the living-room of the little house.

She opened the attack with the desperate courage which is in all mothers when they think for their children, howsoever mean the thoughts may be.

'Ye two men, ye're both in love with my Sarah!'

Their bashful silence gave consent to the barefaced proposition. She went on.

'Neither of ye has much!' Again they tacitly acquiesced in the soft impeachment.

'I don't know that either of ye could keep a wife!' Though neither said a word their looks and bearing expressed distinct dissent. Mrs Trefusis went on: 'But if ye'd put what ye both have together ye'd make a comfortable home for one of ye – and Sarah!' She eyed the men keenly, with her cunning eyes half shut, as she spoke; then satisfied from her scrutiny that the idea was accepted she went on quickly, as if to prevent argument: 'The girl likes ye both, and mayhap it's hard for her to choose. Why don't ye toss up for her? First put your money together – ye've each got a bit put by, I know. Let the lucky man take the lot and trade with it a bit, and then come home and marry her. Neither of ye's afraid, I suppose! And neither of ye'll say that he won't do that much for the girl that ye both say ye love!'

Abel broke the silence: 'It don't seem the square thing to toss for the girl! She wouldn't like it herself, and it doesn't seem – seem respectful like to her –'

Eric interrupted. He was conscious that his chance was not so good as Abel's in case Sarah should wish to choose between them: 'Are ye afraid of the hazard?'

'Not me!' said Abel, boldly. Mrs Trefusis, seeing that her

idea was beginning to work, followed up the advantage.

'It is settled that ye put yer money together to make a home for her, whether ye toss for her or leave it for her to choose?'

'Yes,' said Eric quickly, and Abel agreed with equal sturdiness. Mrs Trefusis' little cunning eyes twinkled. She heard Sarah's step in the yard, and said: 'Well! here she comes, and I leave it to her.' And she went out.

During her brief walk on the hillside Sarah had been trying to make up her mind. She was feeling almost angry with both men for being the cause of her difficulty, and as she came into the room said shortly: 'I want to have a word with you both – come to the Flagstaff Rock, where we can be alone.' She took her hat and went out of the house up the winding path to the steep rock crowned with a high flagstaff, where once the wreckers' fire basket used to burn. This was the rock which formed the northern jaw of the little harbour. There was only room on the path for two abreast, and it marked the state of things pretty well when, by a sort of implied arrangement, Sarah went first, and the two men followed, walking abreast and keeping step. By this time, each man's heart was boiling with jealousy. When they came to the top of the rock, Sarah stood against the flagstaff, and the two young men stood opposite her. She had chosen her position with knowledge and intention, for there was no room for anyone to stand beside her.

They were all silent for a while; then Sarah began to laugh and said: 'I promised the both of you to give you an answer today. I've been thinking and thinking and thinking, till I began to get angry with you both for plaguing me so; and even now I don't seem any nearer than ever I was to making up my mind.'

Eric said suddenly: 'Let us toss for it, lass!'

Sarah showed no indignation whatever at the proposition; her mother's eternal suggestion had schooled her to the acceptance of something of the kind, and her weak nature made it easy to her to grasp at any way out of the difficulty. She stood with downcast eyes idly picking at the sleeve of her dress, seeming to have tacitly acquiesced in the proposal. Both men instinctively realising this pulled each a coin from his pocket, spun it in the air, and dropped his other hand over the palm on which it lay. For a few seconds they remained thus, all silent; then Abel, who was the more thoughtful of the men, spoke: 'Sarah! is this good?' As he spoke he removed the upper hand from the coin and placed the latter back in his pocket. Sarah was nettled.

'Good or bad, it's good enough for me! Take it or leave it as you like,' she said, to which he replied quickly: 'Nay lass! Aught that concerns you is good enow for me. I did but think of you lest you might have pain or disappointment hereafter. If you love Eric better nor me, in God's name say so, and I think I'm man enow to stand aside. Likewise, if I'm the one, don't make us both miserable for life!' Face to face with a difficulty, Sarah's weak nature proclaimed itself; she put her hands before her face and began to cry, saying: 'It was my mother. She keeps telling me!'

The silence which followed was broken by Eric, who said hotly to Abel: 'Let the lass alone, can't you? If she wants to choose this way, let her. It's good enough for me – and for you, too! She's said it now, and must abide by it!'

Hereupon Sarah turned upon him in sudden fury, and cried: 'Hold your tongue! what is it to you, at any rate?' and she resumed her crying. Eric was so flabbergasted that he had not a word to say, but stood looking particularly foolish, with his mouth open and his hands held out with the coin still between them. All were silent till Sarah, taking her hands from her face laughed hysterically and said: 'As you two can't make up your minds, I'm going home!' and she turned to go.

'Stop,' said Abel, in an authoritative voice. 'Eric, you hold the coin, and I'll cry. Now, before we settle it, let us clearly understand: the man who wins takes all the money that we both have got, brings it to Bristol and ships on a voyage and trades with it. Then he comes back and marries Sarah, and they two keep all, whatever there may be, as the result of the trading. Is this what we understand?'

'Yes,' said Eric.

'I'll marry him on my next birthday,' said Sarah. Having said it the intolerably mercenary spirit of her action seemed to strike her, and impulsively she turned away with a bright blush. Fire seemed to sparkle in the eyes of both men. Said Eric: 'A year so be! The man that wins is to have one year.'

'Toss!' cried Abel, and the coin spun in the air. Eric caught it, and again held it between his outstretched hands.

'Heads!' cried Abel, a pallor sweeping over his face as he spoke. As he leaned forward to look Sarah leaned forward too, and their heads almost touched. He could feel her hair blowing on his cheek, and it thrilled through him like fire. Eric lifted his upper band; the coin lay with its head up. Abel stepped forward and took Sarah in his arms. With a curse Eric hurled the coin far into the sea. Then he leaned against the flagstaff and scowled at the others with his hands thrust deep into his pockets. Abel whispered wild words of passion and delight into Sarah's ears, and as she listened she began to believe that fortune had rightly interpreted the wishes of her secret heart, and that she loved Abel best.

Presently Abel looked up and caught sight of Eric's face as the last ray of sunset struck it. The red light intensified the natural ruddiness of his complexion, and he looked as though he were steeped in blood. Abel did not mind his scowl, for now that his own heart was at rest he could feel unalloyed pity for his friend. He stepped over meaning to comfort him, and held out his hand, saying: 'It was my chance, old lad. Don't grudge it me. I'll try to make Sarah a happy woman, and you shall be a brother to us both!'

'Brother be damned!' was all the answer Eric made, as he turned away. When he had gone a few steps down the rocky path he turned and came back. Standing before Abel and Sarah, who had their arms round each other, he said: 'You have a year. Make the most of it! And be sure you're in time to claim your wife! Be back to have your banns up in time to be married on the 11th April. If you're not, I tell you I shall have my banns up, and you may get back too late.'

'What do you mean, Eric? You are mad!'

'No more mad than you are, Abel Behenna. You go, that's your chance! I stay, that's mine! I don't mean to let the grass grow under my feet. Sarah cared no more for you than for me five minutes ago, and she may come back to that five minutes after you're gone! You won by a point only – the game may change.'

'The game won't change!' said Abel shortly. 'Sarah, you'll be true to me? You won't marry till I return?'

'For a year!' added Eric, quickly, 'that's the bargain.'

'I promise for the year,' said Sarah. A dark look came over Abel's face, and he was about to speak, but he mastered himself and smiled.

'I mustn't be too hard or get angry tonight! Come, Eric! we played and fought together. I won fairly. I played fairly all the game of our wooing! You know that as well as I do; and now when I am going away, I shall look to my old and true comrade to help me when I am gone!'

'I'll help you none,' said Eric, 'so help me God!'

'It was God helped me,' said Abel simply.

'Then let Him go on helping you,' said Eric angrily. 'The Devil is good enough for me!' and without another word he rushed down the steep path and disappeared behind the rocks.

When he had gone Abel hoped for some tender passage with Sarah, but the first remark she made chilled him.

'How lonely it all seems without Eric!' and this note sounded till he had left her at home – and after.

Early on the next morning Abel heard a noise at his door, and on going out saw Eric walking rapidly away: a small canvas bag full of gold and silver lay on the threshold; on a small slip of paper pinned to it was written: 'Take the money and go. I stay. God for you! The Devil for me! Remember the 11th of April. ERIC SANSON'.

That afternoon Abel went off to Bristol, and a week later sailed on the *Star of the Sea* bound for Pahang. His money – including that which had been Eric's – was on board in the shape of a venture of cheap toys. He had been advised by a shrewd old mariner of Bristol whom he knew, and who knew the ways of the Chersonese, who predicted that every penny invested would be returned with a shilling to boot.

As the year wore on Sarah became more and more disturbed in her mind. Eric was always at hand to make love to her in his own persistent, masterful manner, and to this she did not object. Only one letter came from Abel, to say that his venture had proved successful, and that he had sent some two hundred pounds to the bank at Bristol, and was trading with fifty pounds still remaining in goods for China, whither the *Star of the Sea* was bound and whence she would return to Bristol. He suggested that Eric's share of the venture should be returned to him with his share of the profits. This proposition was treated with anger by Eric, and as simply childish by Sarah's mother.

More than six months had since then elapsed, but no other letter had come, and Eric's hopes which had been dashed down by the letter from Pahang, began to rise again. He perpetually assailed Sarah with an 'if!' If Abel did not return, would she then marry him? If the 11th April went by without Abel being in the port, would she give him over? If Abel had taken his fortune, and married another girl on the head of it, would she marry him, Eric, as soon as the truth were known? And so on in an endless variety of possibilities.

The power of the strong will and the determined purpose over the woman's weaker nature became in time manifest. Sarah began to lose her faith in Abel and to regard Eric as a possible husband; and a possible husband is in a woman's eye different to all other men. A new affection for him began to arise in her breast, and the daily familiarities of permitted courtship furthered the growing affection. Sarah began to regard Abel as rather a rock in the road of her life, and had it not been for her mother's constantly reminding her of the good fortune already laid by in the Bristol Bank she would have tried to have shut her eyes altogether to the fact of Abel's existence.

The 11th April was Saturday, so that in order to have the marriage on that day it would be necessary that the banns should be called on Sunday, 22nd March. From the beginning of that month Eric kept perpetually on the subject of Abel's absence, and his outspoken opinion that the latter was either dead or married began to become a reality to the woman's mind. As the first half of the month wore on Eric became more jubilant, and after church on the 15th he took Sarah for a walk to the Flagstaff Rock. There he asserted himself strongly: 'I told Abel, and you too, that if he was not here to put up his banns in time for the eleventh, I would put up mine for the twelfth. Now the time has come when I mean to do it. He hasn't kept his word' – here Sarah struck in out

21

of her weakness and indecision: 'He hasn't broken it yet!' Eric ground his teeth with anger.

'If you mean to stick up for him,' he said, as he smote his hands savagely on the flagstaff, which sent forth a shivering murmur, 'well and good. I'll keep my part of the bargain. On Sunday I shall give notice of the banns, and you can deny them in the church if you will. If Abel is in Pencastle on the eleventh, he can have them cancelled, and his own put up; but till then, I take my course, and woe to anyone who stands in my way!' With that he flung himself down the rocky pathway, and Sarah could not but admire his Viking strength and spirit, as, crossing the hill, he strode away along the cliffs towards Bude.

During the week no news was heard of Abel, and on Saturday Eric gave notice of the banns of marriage between himself and Sarah Trefusis. The clergyman would have remonstrated with him, for although nothing formal had been told to the neighbours, it had been understood since Abel's departure that on his return he was to marry Sarah; but Eric would not discuss the question.

'It is a painful subject, sir,' he said with a firmness which the parson, who was a very young man, could not but be swayed by. 'Surely there is nothing against Sarah or me. Why should there be any bones made about the matter?' The parson said no more, and on the next day he read out the banns for the first time amidst an audible buzz from the congregation. Sarah was present, contrary to custom, and though she blushed furiously enjoyed her triumph over the other girls whose banns had not yet come. Before the week was over she began to make her wedding dress. Eric used to come and look at her at work and the sight thrilled through him. He used to say all sorts of pretty things to her at such times, and there were to both delicious moments of love-making.

The banns were read a second time on the 29th, and Eric's hope grew more and more fixed though there were to him moments of acute despair when he realised that the cup of happiness might be dashed from his lips at any moment, right up to the last. At such times he was full of passion – desperate and remorseless – and he ground his teeth and clenched his hands in a wild way as though some taint of the old Berserker fury of his ancestors still lingered in his blood. On the Thursday of that week he looked in on Sarah and found her, amid a flood of sunshine, putting finishing touches to her white wedding gown. His own heart was full of gaiety, and the sight of the woman who was so soon to be his own so occupied, filled him with a joy unspeakable, and he felt faint with languorous ecstasy. Bending over he kissed Sarah on the mouth, and then whispered in her rosy ear – 'Your wedding dress, Sarah! And for me!'

As he drew back to admire her she looked up saucily, and said to him – 'Perhaps not for you. There is more than a week yet for Abel!' and then cried out in dismay, for with a wild gesture and a fierce oath Eric dashed out of the house, banging the door behind him. The incident disturbed Sarah more than she could have thought possible, for it awoke all her fears and doubts and indecision afresh. She cried a little, and put by her dress, and to soothe herself went out to sit for a while on the summit of the Flagstaff Rock. When she arrived she found there a little group anxiously discussing the weather. The sea was calm and the sun bright, but across the sea were strange lines of darkness and light, and close in to shore the rocks were fringed with foam, which spread out in great white curves and circles as the currents drifted. The wind had backed, and came in sharp, cold puffs. The blow-hole, which ran under the Flagstaff Rock, from the rocky bay without to the harbour within, was booming at intervals, and the seagulls were screaming ceaselessly as they wheeled about the entrance of the port.

'It looks bad,' she heard an old fisherman say to the coastguard. 'I seen it just like this once before, when the East Indiaman *Coromandel* went to pieces in Dizzard Bay!' Sarah did not wait to hear more. She was of a timid nature where danger was concerned, and could not bear to hear of wrecks and disasters. She went home and resumed the completion of her dress, secretly determined to appease Eric when she should meet him with a sweet apology – and to take the earliest opportunity of being even with him after her marriage.

The old fisherman's weather prophecy was justified. That night at dusk a wild storm came on. The sea rose and lashed the western coasts from Skye to Scilly and left a tale of disaster everywhere. The sailors and fishermen of Pencastle all turned out on the rocks and cliffs and watched eagerly. Presently, by a flash of lightning, a 'ketch' was seen drifting under only a jib about half-a-mile outside the port. All eyes and all glasses were concentrated on her, waiting for the next flash, and when it came a chorus went up that it was the *Lovely Alice*, trading between Bristol and Penzance, and touching at all the little ports between. 'God help them!' said the harbourmaster, 'for nothing in this world can save them when they are between Bude and Tintagel and the wind on shore!' The coastguards exerted themselves, and, aided by brave hearts and willing hands, they brought the rocket apparatus up on the summit of the Flagstaff Rock. Then they burned blue lights so that those on board might see the harbour opening in case they could make any effort to reach it. They worked gallantly enough on board; but no skill or strength of man could avail. Before many minutes were over the *Lovely Alice* rushed to her doom on the great island rock that guarded the mouth of the port. The screams of those on board were faintly borne on the tempest as they flung themselves into the sea in a last chance for life. The blue lights were kept burning, and eager eyes peered into the depths of the waters in case any face could be seen; and ropes were held ready to fling out in aid. But never a face was seen, and the willing arms rested idle. Eric was there amongst his fellows. His old Icelandic origin was never more apparent than in that wild hour. He took a rope, and shouted in the ear of the harbour-master: 'I shall go down on the rock over the seal cave. The tide is running up, and someone may drift in there!'

'Keep back, man!' came the answer. 'Are you mad? One slip on that rock and you are lost: and no man could keep his feet in the dark on such a place in such a tempest!'

'Not a bit,' came the reply. 'You remember how Abel Behenna saved me there on a night like this when my boat went on the Gull Rock. He dragged me up from the deep water in the seal cave, and now someone may drift in there again as I did,' and he was gone into the darkness. The projecting rock hid the light on the Flagstaff Rock, but he knew his way too well to miss it. His boldness and sureness of foot standing to him, he shortly stood on the great round-topped rock cut away beneath by the action of the waves over the entrance of the seal cave, where the water was fathomless. There he stood in comparative safety, for the concave shape of the rock beat back the waves with their own force, and though the water below him seemed to boil like a seething cauldron, just beyond the spot there was a space of almost calm. The rock, too, seemed here to shut off the sound of the gale, and he listened as well as watched. As he stood there ready, with his coil of rope poised to throw, he thought he heard below him, just beyond the whirl of the water, a faint, despairing cry. He echoed it with a shout that rang into the night. Then he waited for the flash of lightning, and as it passed flung his rope out into the darkness where he had seen a face rising through the swirl of the foam. The rope was caught, for he felt a pull on it, and he shouted again in his mighty voice: 'Tie it round your waist, and I shall pull you up.' Then when he felt that it was fast he moved along the rock to the far side of the sea cave, where the deep water was something stiller, and where he could get foothold secure enough to drag the rescued man on the overhanging rock. He began to pull, and shortly he knew from the rope taken in that the man he was now rescuing must soon be close to the top of the rock. He steadied himself for a moment, and drew a long breath, that he might at the next effort complete the rescue. He had just bent his back to the work when a flash of lightning revealed to each other the two men – the rescuer and the rescued.

Eric Sanson and Abel Behenna were face to face – and none knew of the meeting save themselves; and God.

On the instant a wave of passion swept through Eric's heart. All his hopes were shattered, and with the hatred of Cain his eyes looked out. He saw in the instant of recognition the joy in Abel's face that his was the hand to succour him, and this intensified his hate. Whilst the passion was on him he started back, and the rope ran out between his hands. His moment of hate was followed by an impulse of his better manhood, but it was too late.

Before he could recover himself, Abel, encumbered with the rope that should have aided him, was plunged with a despairing cry back into the darkness of the devouring sea.

Then, feeling all the madness and the doom of Cain upon him, Eric rushed back over the rocks, heedless of the danger and eager only for one thing – to be amongst other people whose living noises would shut out that last cry which seemed to ring still in his ears. When he regained the Flagstaff Rock the men surrounded him, and through the fury of the storm he heard the harbour-master say: 'We feared you were lost when we heard a cry! How white you are! Where is your rope? Was there anyone drifted in?'

'No one,' he shouted in answer, for he felt that he could never explain that he had let his old comrade slip back into the sea, and at the very place and under the very circumstances in which that comrade had saved his own life. He hoped by one bold lie to set the matter at rest for ever. There was no one to bear witness – and if he should have to carry that still white face in his eyes and that despairing cry in his ears for evermore – at least none should know of it. 'No one,' he cried, more loudly still. 'I slipped on the rock, and the rope fell into the sea!' So saying he left them, and, rushing down the steep path, gained his own cottage and locked himself within.

The remainder of that night he passed lying on his bed – dressed and motionless – staring upwards, and seeming to see through the darkness a pale face gleaming wet in the lightning, with its glad recognition turning to ghastly despair, and to hear a cry which never ceased to echo in his soul.

In the morning the storm was over and all was smiling again, except that the sea was still boisterous with its unspent fury. Great pieces of wreck drifted into the port, and the sea around the island rock was strewn with others. Two bodies also drifted into the harbour – one the master of the wrecked ketch, the other a strange seaman whom no one knew.

Sarah saw nothing of Eric till the evening, and then he only looked in for a minute. He did not come into the house, but simply put his head in through the open window.

'Well, Sarah,' he called out in a loud voice, though to her it did not ring truly, 'is the wedding dress done? Sunday week, mind! Sunday week!'

Sarah was glad to have the reconciliation so easy; but, womanlike, when she saw the storm was over and her own fears groundless, she at once repeated the cause of offence.

'Sunday so be it,' she said without looking up, 'if Abel isn't there on Saturday!' Then she looked up saucily, though her heart was full of fear of another outburst on the part of her impetuous lover. But the window was empty; Eric had taken himself off, and with a pout she resumed her work. She saw Eric no more till Sunday afternoon, after the banns had been called the third time, when he came up to her before all the people with an air of proprietorship which half-pleased and half-annoyed her.

'Not yet, mister!' she said, pushing him away, as the other girls giggled. 'Wait till Sunday next, if you please – the day after Saturday!' she added, looking at him saucily. The girls giggled again, and the young men guffawed. They thought it was the snub that touched him so that he became as white as a sheet as he turned away. But Sarah, who knew more than they did, laughed, for she saw triumph through the spasm of pain that overspread his face.

The week passed uneventfully; however, as Saturday drew nigh Sarah had occasional moments of anxiety, and as to Eric he went about at night-time like a man possessed. He restrained himself when others were by, but now and again he went down amongst the rocks and caves and shouted aloud.

This seemed to relieve him somewhat, and he was better able to restrain himself for some time after. All Saturday he stayed in his own house and never left it. As he was to be married on the morrow, the neighbours thought it was shyness on his part, and did not trouble or notice him.

Only once was he disturbed, and that was when the chief boatman came to him and sat down, and after a pause said: 'Eric, I was over in Bristol yesterday. I was in the ropemaker's getting a coil to replace the one you lost the night of the storm, and there I saw Michael Heavens of this place, who is a salesman there. He told me that Abel Behenna had come home the week ere last on the *Star of the Sea* from Canton, and that he had lodged a sight of money in the Bristol Bank in the name of Sarah Behenna. He told Michael so himself – and that he had taken passage on the *Lovely Alice* to Pencastle. Bear up, man,' for Eric had with a groan dropped his head on his knees, with his face between his hands. 'He was your old comrade, I know, but you couldn't help him. He must have gone down with the rest that awful night. I thought I'd better tell you, lest it might come some other way, and you might keep Sarah Trefusis from being frightened. They were good friends once, and women take these things to heart. It would not do to let her be pained with such a thing on her wedding day!' Then he rose and went away, leaving Eric still sitting disconsolately with his head on his knees.

'Poor fellow!' murmured the chief boatman to himself; 'he takes it to heart. Well, well! right enough! They were true comrades once, and Abel saved him!'

The afternoon of that day, when the children had left school, they strayed as usual on half-holidays along the quay and the paths by the cliffs. Presently some of them came running in a state of great excitement to the harbour, where a few men were unloading a coal ketch, and a great many were superintending the operation. One of the children called out: 'There is a porpoise in the harbour mouth! We saw it come through the blow-hole! It had a long tail, and was deep under the water!'

'It was no porpoise,' said another; 'it was a seal; but it had a long tail! It came out of the seal cave!' The other children bore various testimony, but on two points they were unanimous – it, whatever 'it' was, had come through the blow-hole deep under the water, and had a long, thin tail – a tail so long that they could not see the end of it. There was much unmerciful chaffing of the children by the men on this point, but as it was evident that they had seen something, quite a number of persons, young and old, male and female, went along the high paths on either side of the harbour mouth to catch a glimpse of this new addition to the fauna of the sea, a long-tailed porpoise or seal. The tide was now coming in. There was a slight breeze, and the surface of the water was rippled so that it was only at moments that anyone could see clearly into the deep water. After a spell of watching a woman called out that she saw something moving up the channel, just below where she was standing. There was a stampede to the spot, but by the time the crowd had gathered the breeze had freshened, and it was impossible to see with any distinctness below the surface of the water. On being questioned the woman described what she had seen, but in such an incoherent way that the whole thing was put down as an effect of imagination; had it not been for the children's report she would not have been credited at all. Her semi-hysterical statement that what she saw was 'like a pig with the entrails out' was only thought anything of by an old coastguard, who shook his head but did not make any remark. For the remainder of the daylight this man was seen always on the bank, looking into the water, but always with disappointment manifest on his face.

Eric arose early on the next morning – he had not slept all night, and it was a relief to him to move about in the light. He shaved himself with a hand that did not tremble, and dressed himself in his wedding clothes. There was a haggard look on his face, and he seemed as though he had grown years older in the last few days. Still there was a wild, uneasy light of triumph in his eyes, and he kept murmuring to himself over and over again: 'This is my wedding-day! Abel cannot claim

her now – living or dead! – living or dead! Living or dead!'
He sat in his armchair, waiting with an uncanny quietness
for the church hour to arrive.

When the bell began to ring he arose and passed out of
his house, closing the door behind him. He looked at the
river and saw the tide had just turned. In the church he sat
with Sarah and her mother, holding Sarah's hand tightly in
his all the time, as though he feared to lose her. When the
service was over they stood up together, and were married
in the presence of the entire congregation; for no one left
the church. Both made the responses clearly – Eric's being
even on the defiant side. When the wedding was over Sarah
took her husband's arm, and they walked away together, the
boys and younger girls being cuffed by their elders into a
decorous behaviour, for they would fain have followed close
behind their heels.

The way from the church led down to the back of Eric's
cottage, a narrow passage being between it and that of his
next neighbour. When the bridal couple had passed through
this the remainder of the congregation, who had followed
them at a little distance, were startled by a long, shrill scream
from the bride. They rushed through the passage and found
her on the bank with wild eyes, pointing to the river bed
opposite Eric Sanson's door.

The falling tide had deposited there the body of Abel

Behenna stark upon the broken rocks. The rope trailing from its waist had been twisted by the current round the mooring post, and had held it back whilst the tide had ebbed away from it. The right elbow had fallen in a chink in the rock, leaving the hand outstretched toward Sarah, with the open palm upward as though it were extended to receive hers, the pale drooping fingers open to the clasp.

All that happened afterwards was never quite known to Sarah Sanson. Whenever she would try to recollect there would become a buzzing in her ears and a dimness in her eyes, and all would pass away. The only thing that she could remember of it all – and this she never forgot – was Eric's breathing heavily, with his face whiter than that of the dead man, as he muttered under his breath: 'Devil's help! Devil's faith! Devil's price!'

ROBERT E. HOWARD

Robert Ervin Howard was born in Peaster, Texas in 1906. During his youth, his family moved between a variety of Texan boomtowns, and Howard – a bookish and somewhat introverted child – was steeped in the violent myths and legends of the Old South. Although he loved reading and learning, Howard developed a distinctly Texan, hardboiled outlook on the world. He became a passionate fan of boxing, taking it up at an amateur level, and from the age of nine began to write adventure tales of semi-historical bloodshed. In 1919, when Howard was thirteen, his family moved to the Central Texas hamlet of Cross Plains, where he would stay for the rest of his life.

At fifteen Howard began to read the pulp magazines of the day, and to write more seriously. The December 1922 issue of his high school newspaper featured two of his stories, 'Golden Hope Christmas' and 'West is West'. In 1924 he sold his first piece – a short caveman tale titled 'Spear and Fang' – for $16 to the not-yet-famous *Weird Tales* magazine. He published with the magazine regularly over the next few years. 1929 was a breakout year for Howard, in that the 23-year-old writer began to sell to other magazines, such as *Ghost Stories* and *Argosy*, both of whom had previously sent him hundreds of rejection slips. In 1930, he began a correspondence with weird fiction master H. P. Lovecraft which ran up to his death six years later, and is regarded as one of the great correspondence cycles in all of fantasy literature.

It was partly due to Lovecraft's encouragement that Howard created his most famous character, Conan the Cimmerian. Conan – a barbarian-turned-King during the Hyborian Age, a mythical period of some 12,000 years ago – featured in seventeen *Weird Tales* stories between 1933 and 1936, and is now regarded as having spawned the 'sword and sorcery' genre, making Howard's influence on fantasy literature comparable to that of J. R. R. Tolkien's. The Conan stories have since been adapted many times, most famously in the series of films starring Arnold Schwarzenegger.

Howard was enjoying an all-time high in sales by the beginning of 1936, but he was also deeply upset by the ill health of his mother, who had fallen into a coma. On the morning of June 11, 1936, he asked an attending nurse whether she would ever recover, and the nurse replied negatively. Howard walked to his car, parked outside the family home in Cross Plains, and shot himself. He died eight hours later, aged just thirty.

THE LITTLE PEOPLE

ROBERT E. HOWARD

My sister threw down the book she was reading. To be exact, she threw it at me.

'Foolishness!' said she. 'Fairy tales! Hand me that copy of Michael Arlen.'

I did so mechanically, glancing at the volume which had incurred her youthful displeasure. The story was *The Shining Pyramid* by Arthur Machen.

'My dear girl,' said I, 'this is a masterpiece of *outre* literature.'

'Yes, but the idea!' she answered. 'I outgrew fairy tales when I was ten.'

'This tale is not intended to be an exponent of common-day realism,' I explained patiently.

'Too far-fetched,' she said, with the finality of seventeen. 'I like to read about things that could happen – who were "The Little People" he speaks of – the same old elf and troll business?'

'All legends have a base of fact,' I said. 'There is a reason. . . .'

'You mean to tell me such things actually existed?' she exclaimed. 'Rot!'

'Not so fast young lady,' I admonished, slightly nettled. 'I mean that all myths had a concrete beginning which was later changed and twisted so as to take on a supernatural significance. Young people,' I continued, bending a brotherly frown on her pouting lips, 'have a way of either accepting entirely or rejecting entirely such things as they do not understand. The "Little People" spoken of by Machen are supposed to be descendants of the prehistoric people who inhabited Europe before the Celts came down out of the north.

'They are known variously as Turanians, Picts, Mediterraneans, and Garlic Eaters. A race of small dark people, traces of their type may be found in primitive sections of Europe and Asia today, among the Basques of Spain, the Scots of Galloway, and the Lapps.

'They were workers in flint and are known to anthropologists as men of the Neolithic, or polished stone, age. Relics of their age show plainly that they had reached a comparatively high stage of primitive culture by the beginning of the bronze age, which was ushered in by the ancestors of the Celts – our prehistoric tribesmen, young lady.

'These destroyed or enslaved the Mediterranean peoples and were in turn ousted by the Teutonic tribes. All over Europe, and especially in Britain, the legend is that these Picts, whom the Celts looked upon as scarcely human, fled to caverns under the earth and lived there, coming out only at night, when they would burn, murder, and carry off children for their bloody rites of worship. Doubtless there was much in this theory. Descendants of cave people, these fleeing dwarves would no doubt take refuge in caverns and no doubt managed to live undiscovered for generations.'

'That was a long time ago,' she said with slight interest. 'If there were ever any of those people, they are dead now. Why, we're right in the country where they're supposed to perform, and we haven't seen any signs of them.'

I nodded. My sister Joan did not react to the weird West country as I did. The immense menhirs and cromlechs which rose starkly upon the moors seemed to bring back vague memories, stirring my Celtic imagination.

'Maybe,' I said, adding unwisely, 'You heard what that old villager said: the warning about walking on the fen at night No one does it. You're very sophisticated, young lady, but I'll bet you wouldn't spend a night alone in that stone ruin we can see from my window.'

Down came her book and her eyes sparkled with interest. 'I'll do it!' she exclaimed. 'I'll show you! He did say no one would go near those old rocks at night, didn't he? I will, and stay there the rest of the night!'

She was on her feet instantly, and I saw that I had made a mistake.

'No you won't, either,' I vetoed. 'What would people think?'

'What do I care what they think?' she retorted in the up-to-date spirit of the Younger Generation.

'You haven't any business out on the moors at night,' I answered. 'Granting that these old myths are so much empty wind, there are plenty of shady characters who wouldn't hesitate to harm a helpless girl. It's not safe for a girl like you to be out unprotected.'

'You mean I'm too pretty?' she asked naïvely.

'I mean you're too foolish,' I answered in my best older brother manner.

She made a face at me and was silent for a moment, and I who could read her agile mind with absurd ease, could tell by her pensive features and sparkling eyes exactly what she was thinking. She was mentally surrounded by a crowd of her cronies back home, and I could guess the exact words which she was already framing: 'My dears, I spent a whole night in the most romantic old ruin in West England, which was supposed to be haunted –'

I silently cursed myself for bringing the subject up, when

she said abruptly; 'I'm going to do it, just the same. Nobody will harm me, and I wouldn't pass up the adventure for anything!'

'Joan,' said, 'I forbid you to go out alone tonight or any other night.'

Her eyes flashed, and I instantly wished I had couched my command in more tactful language. My sister was wilful and high-spirited, used to having her way and very impatient of restraint.

'You can't order me around,' she flamed. 'You've done nothing but bully me ever since we left America.'

'It's been necessary,' I sighed. 'I can think of a number of pastimes more pleasant than touring Europe with a flapper sister.'

Her mouth opened as if to reply angrily; then she shrugged her slim shoulders and settled back down in her chair, taking up a book.

'All right, I didn't want to go much anyhow,' she remarked casually. I eyed her suspiciously; she was not usually subdued so easily. In fact, some of the most harrowing moments of my life have been those in which I was forced to cajole and coax her out of a rebellious mood.

Nor was my suspicion entirely vanquished when, a few moments later, she announced her intention of retiring, and went to her room just across the corridor.

I turned out the light and stepped over to my window, which opened upon a wide view of the barren, undulating wastes of the moor. The moon was just rising, and the land glimmered grisly and stark beneath its cold beams. It was late summer and the air was warm, yet the whole landscape looked cold, bleak and forbidding. Across the fen I saw rise, stark and shadowy, the rough and mighty spires of the ruined cromlech. Gaunt and terrible, they loomed against the night, silent phantoms from the past.

Sleep did not come to me at once, for I was hurt at my sister's evident resentment, and I lay for a long time, brooding and staring at the window, now framed boldly in the molten silver of the moon. At length I dropped into a troubled slumber, through which flitted vague dreams wherein dim, ghostly shapes glided and leered.

I awoke suddenly, sat up and stared about me wildly, striving to orientate my muddled senses. An oppressive feeling as of impending evil hovered about me. Fading swiftly as I came to full consciousness, lurked the eery remembrance of a hazy dream wherein a white fog had floated through the window and had assumed the shape of a tall, white-bearded man who had shaken my shoulder as if to arouse me from sleep. All of us are familiar with the curious sensations of waking from a bad dream – the dimming and dwindling of partly remembered thoughts and feelings. But the wider awake I became, the stronger grew the suggestion of evil.

I sprang up, snatched on my clothing, and rushed to my sister's room and flung open the door. The room was unoccupied.

I raced down the stairs and accosted the night clerk who was maintained by the small hotel for some obscure reason.

'Miss Costigan, sir? She came down, clad for outdoors, a while after midnight – about half an hour ago, sir, and said she was going to take a stroll on the moor and not to be alarmed if she did not return at once, sir.'

I hurled myself out of the hotel, my pulse pounding a devil's tattoo. Far out across the fen I saw the ruins, bold and grim against the moon, and in that direction I hastened. At length – it seemed hours – I saw a slim figure some distance in front of me. The girl was taking her time and in spite of her start on me, I was gaining – she soon would be within hearing distance. My breath was already coming in gasps from my exertions, but I quickened my pace.

The aura of the fen was like a tangible presence, pressing upon me, weighting my limbs – and always that presentiment of evil grew and grew.

Then, far ahead of me, I saw my sister stop suddenly and look about confusedly. The moonlight flung a veil of illusion; I could see her, but I could not see what caused her sudden terror. I broke into a run, my blood leaping wildly and suddenly freezing as a wild, despairing scream burst out and sent the echoes flying.

The girl was turning first one way and then another, and I screamed for her to run toward me. She heard me and started toward me, running like a frightened antelope – and then I *saw*. Vague shadows darted about her, short, dwarfish shapes; just in front of me rose a solid wall of them, and I saw that they had blocked her from gaining to me. Suddenly, instinctively I believe, she turned and raced for the stone columns, the whole horde after her, save those who remained to bar my path.

I had no weapon, nor did I feel the need for any. A strong, athletic youth, I was in addition an amateur boxer of ability, with a terrific punch in either hand. Now all the primal instincts surged in me. I was a cave man bent on vengeance against a tribe which sought to steal a woman of my family. I did not fear; I only wished to close with them. Aye, though the whole spawn of Hell rise up from those caverns which honeycomb the moors. Aye, I recognised these – I knew them of old, and all the old wars rose and roared within the misty caverns of my soul. Hate leaped in me as in the old days when men of my blood came from the North.

Now I was almost upon those who barred my way. I saw plainly the stunted bodies, the gnarled limbs, the beady reptilian eyes that stared unwinkingly, the grotesque, square faces with their inhuman features, and the shimmer of flint daggers in their crooked hands. Then with a tigerish leap I was among them like a leopard among jackals, and details were blotted out in a whirling red haze. Whatever they were, they were of living substance; features crumpled and bones shattered beneath my flailing fists and blood darkened the moon-silvered stones. A flint dagger sank hilt deep in my thigh. Then the ghastly throng broke each way and fled before me, as their ancestors fled before mine, leaving four silent dwarfish shapes stretched on the moor.

Heedless of my wound, I took up the grim race anew. Joan had reached the druidic ruins now, and she leaned against one of the columns, exhausted, blindly seeking there the protection in obedience to some dim instinct, just as women of her blood had done in bygone ages.

The horrid beings that pursued her were closing in upon her. They would reach her before I. God knows the thing was horrible enough, but back in the recesses of my mind, grimmer horrors were whispering: dream memories wherein stunted creatures pursues white-limbed women across such fens as these. Lurking memories of the ages when dawns were young and men struggled with forces which were not of men.

The girl toppled forward in a faint, and lay at the foot of the towering column in a piteous white heap. And they closed in – closed in. What they would do I knew not, but the ghosts of ancient memory whispered that they would do something of hideous evil, something foul and grim.

From my lips burst a scream, wild and inarticulate, born of sheer elemental horror and despair. I could not reach her before those fiends had worked their frightful will upon her. The centuries, the ages swept back. This was it as it had been in the beginning. And what followed, I know not how to explain, but I think that that wild shriek whispered back down the long reaches of Time to the Beings my ancestors worshipped, and that blood answered blood. Aye, such a shriek as could echo down the dusty corridors of lost ages and bring back from the whispering abyss of Eternity the ghost of the only one who could save a girl of Celtic blood.

The foremost of the beings were almost upon the prostrate girl; their hands were clutching for her, when suddenly beside her a form stood. There was no gradual materialising; the figure leaped suddenly into being, etched bold and clear in the moonlight. A tall, white-bearded man, clad in long robes – the man I had seen in my dream! A druid, answering once more the desperate need of people of his race. His brow was high and noble, his eyes mystic and far-seeing – so much I could see, even from where I ran. His arm rose in an imperious gesture, and the beings shrunk back – back – back –. They broke and fled, vanishing suddenly, and I sank to my knees beside my sister, gathering the child into my arms. A moment I looked up at the man, sword and shield against the powers of darkness, as in the world's youth. He raised his hand above us as if in benediction; then he too vanished suddenly, and the moor lay bare and silent.

DOROTHY MACARDLE

Dorothy Macardle was born in Dundalk, Ireland in 1889. She attended University College, Dublin, and upon graduating returned to her secondary school to teach English. An active Irish nationalist, Macardle joined a women's paramilitary organisation in 1917, and was arrested during the Irish War of Independence. She recounted her experiences of this time in *Earthbound: Nine Stories of Ireland* (1924), and went on to write a number of plays. In 1937, Macardle published her mammoth work, *The Irish Republic*, now one of the most frequently cited narrative accounts of the Irish War of Independence and its aftermath. She also produced a number of short stories and essays. During the thirties, she worked as a journalist with the League of Nations, and developed a deep concern for the plight of pre-war Czechoslovakia. Macardle was a dedicated political activist right up to her death.

THE UNINVITED

STORY 'SAMHAIN' BY DOROTHY MACARDLE

It was only on rare and premeditated occasions that the studio was visited by Una's old friend Andrew Fitzgerald. He had been burrowing through his great work on Celtic Etymology for so many years that "by the law of inertia," he said, he could not stop. But once or twice in a season he would emerge, blinking, into the light and visit his young friends. He came one April evening to meet Doctor Christiansen, the Norwegian folklorist, and he was as happy as a Leprechaun talking of trolls and pooka and the Sidhe and Norse monuments in Ireland and the ship symbol in Brugh-na-Boinne.

Doctor Christiansen had been exploring the Gaeltacht and was full of delight in the people he had met.

"What is to me most charming," he said, "is their good friendship with their dead. I hoped much to meet a revenant, or a woman of the Sidhe – but alas, to a Norseman, she would not appear!"

Una looked at him reproachfully. "You are laughing at

us," she said.

"Indeed no!" he replied quickly. "I have learned so much, I no longer venture to disbelieve. To me, magics and religions all are one, and all very full with what is true. And those people – they speak in good faith. It was in Kerry, more than anywhere in the world," he went on, "that poor, beautiful country, that they told me mysteries of the dead."

"Still, you thought the people credulous," FitzGerald said gently; "but you will not suspect a lexicographer of being fantastical. I, too, could tell you of strange happenings in Kerry – a mystery of the dead."

"Daddy Fitz!" Frank exclaimed, "how well you never told us you had seen a ghost!"

"But I saw no ghost, Avic," he replied, his crumpled old face sweet with a reminiscent smile. "If I had seen him, I think, truly, I should now be far away. I will tell you, if you like, what I heard."

"If you please!" begged Dr Christiansen eagerly.

"Please!" said Una. "Was it long ago?"

"Long ago indeed – when I was young. I was learning Irish at that time and I went to live in a small fishing village in West Kerry where the people had the language still – and had very little else.

I made the best friend of my life there; 'twas Father Patrick O'Rahilly, the parish priest, a middle-aged man, but white-haired, very delicate – the nearest creature to a saint I have ever known.

No life could be more lonely, I suppose, than that of an Irish priest in those desert regions of the west and south; This man had been a student and traveler in his youth – he had a very subtle, originating mind – and there he was, marooned among the poorest fisher-folk in existence – too poor himself to buy books. My coming, heretic though he found me – I was a sort of agnostic then – was a godsend to him; he made no secret of it from the first, and I was as welcome to the Presbytery as if it had been my home.

I rejoiced in the man and in his queer, desultory house; there was charm, life about it, though 'twas not old. It had been built a generation ago by a Father Howe. He had chosen the site for the sake of the grand view. Over Dingle Bay, you looked, through a gap in the trees, across to the mountains – mountains like mother-o'-pearl. To secure that he did what the folk said was a wrongful thing; he built on an old pathway that ran from the chapel to the ancient graveyard on the hill. That path had been disused altogether since the opening of the military road. He harmed no living soul, building on it; moreover he lived jovially, and died piously in his bed; all the same the people never gave up blaming his choice. "'Twas bad," they said, "to go meddling with an old path; there's them might be wishful to be using it still."

There was one old woman who used to beg Father Patrick with tears in her eyes, every time she met him, to take a house somewhere else. I remember the day his patience gave out.

"Maura O'Shea," he said sternly, "are you suggesting that a priest of God has cause to dread the vengeance of the living or of the dead?"

And "Ah, Father Patrick, dear," she replied in distress, "don't you know we'd stay out of Heaven itself, and Saint Peter bidding us step in, to do a good turn to you, alive or dead?"

They are people who know how to love and to speak out of the heart as well as out of the mind.

My coming brought the bad luck, so it seemed. All that Summer and Autumn one disaster after another broke on those unfortunate people, until, towards Samhain time, the last blow came – Father Patrick fell ill."

"Sah-wen?" Max, repeated enquiringly. His tongue tangled always over Irish words. Dr Christiansen looked up, smiling:

"Your Festival of the Dead?"

"It corresponds, doesn't it, to the Feast of Balor?" FitzGerald went on: "Mananaan, the god of the underworld was potent then and it is a time of strange happenings in Gaelic countries still. It is then, in Ireland, that the living pray for the dead, invoking the prayers of the holy saints; it is then, old people will tell you, that the drowned come up out of the sea – they come to draw away living souls; there are footfalls you must not follow, knocking to which you dare not open; dead voices call . . .

The trouble began about July; 'twas the wettest July Corney O'Grady remembered, and he was ninety-five years old.

August was a month of storm; day after day passed and the little boats dared not venture out, while the pirating French trawlers, hardier vessels, came plundering the spawn-beds – destroying the harvest of the sea. The farms, no more than potato patches among the stones, which were the fisher-folks' last resource, failed them, too; the potatoes came black and rotten from the summer rains.

It was one of those seasons of heart-breaking tragedy which are recurrent on those Irish coasts where the people dwell in the Valley of the Shadow all their lives. By the end of Summer the spectre of famine had come.

I think that but for Father Patrick many of those poor souls would have boarded up their windows, as in the old days, and lain down in their bare huts to die; but he was with them like an inspired and inspiring spirit, giving them courage, energy and hope. He got an instructress from Cork to start a knitting industry and the girls worked hard, but they could get no price for the garments they made. And all the time the sky was pitiless. "You'd think," old Corney said bitterly, "God grudged Ireland the light of the sun."

The men began to get desperate. They saw the children growing wizened and sickly before their eyes. They were without milk, without flour, without even Indian meal. I don't think they cried or complained, the children, but they had not the strength to climb the steep road to the school. You'd see them creeping among the potato ridges, turning over the sods, in the hope that a good potato might remain.

The men took to going out in any weather at all – going twenty miles out to sea in their canoes, and they'd come home without having netted a fish. Many a time, at the pleading of a distracted wife or mother, Father Patrick went down to them to protest, but even he could not hold them now. "Sure, Father," they would answer, "there is death only before us anyway, and isn't it better go look for it on the water than bide waiting it on the black land? What good are we to the childer, and we walking the roads?"

The best boat in the village was owned by a grand old fellow named MacCarthy, his two sons and his son-in-law, Dermot Roche. There was a tribe of young children dependent on this crew, and I watched the demons of misery give place to the demons of recklessness in the sombre eyes of the men.

I troubled most about Dermot. The man attracted me strongly and had taken me under his protection from the first. He was a creature of fierce attachments; he loved me, I think, for my love of the Irish; he never let a word of English across his tongue. To my imagination he incarnated the spirit of that savage, primitive, gentle place; hard and gaunt he was as the rocks, protective as the hills; he seemed to know its terrible history "in his bones." I never saw him smile, but I have seen him glow with a kind of angry joy. He used to take me out fishing in the early morning to teach me the old ranns and proverbs that he knew I loved, and he would sing to me on the water wild old traditional songs in a rich voice that had a drone in it like the wind. He had a shy, smiling little wife, and half-a-dozen black-haired youngsters who seemed to live like sea-creatures among the rocks. Father Patrick had been good to the children, and for Father Patrick, Dermot would have faced the legions of Hell. In those famine days the man's face became terrible; his wife was expecting another child.

I was sitting at the round table in the Presbytery, that black September evening, reading with Father Patrick the ancient annals which were his delight and mine, when Dermot unlatched the door and came striding in – a man angry with his God. Father Patrick's gentle welcome was too much for him; he sat down and laid his head on the table and wept. Annie had given birth to a seventh child and died.

Father Patrick asked me to stay in the house in case any call should come, and went down with Dermot. He came back in the morning worn out, his habitual tranquillity gone.

"The men are losing hold of themselves," he said. "'Tis not right. Dermot's left the neighbors to wake Annie, and gone off with MacCarthy in the boat."

All that day a diabolical gale was raging. The boat did not come home. By dusk the people were huddling together, silent and ghastly, at the little pier; as long as daylight lasted there was nothing visible but the grey, murderous sea. At dawn they launched the life-boat and it came back at noon. Mat Kearney climbed out of it and passed up through the crowd. He answered me with a heavy gesture of his hand: "They're all away." His own son was in it – one of the crew of eight. They had found the boat upside down.

If Father Patrick had laboured before, he laboured after this like forty men; day and night, in wind and wet, he was in and out of the broken hovels, bringing what comfort there was to bring to forlorn old mothers and derelict young widows and starving families that had no man.

I sent an appeal to the Dublin press and to friends in Boston which brought us enough to keep Dermot's orphans and the MacCarthy's for a few weeks; after that, neighbours who had forgotten what it was not to be hungry took the children to their own homes.

Our language studies were all laid aside. When Father

Patrick was not visiting he would be brooding and writing and calculating, trying to work out schemes. He knew little of the commercial world and I thought most of his suggestions impracticable; but one seemed sound. He began corresponding with traders in Cork and Dublin, trying to work up a market for carrigeen moss – a kind of edible seaweed which grows in the rock pools and can be gathered at low tide. He hoped to have a sale for it very soon. It could never, of course, bring in much to the poor creatures, but the work and planning kept them from black despair.

But all the time Father Patrick was struggling against illness, himself obsessed by a fear of breaking down. His people had no one else.

Then, near and far along the coast, washed up by the tide, the bodies of the drowned fishermen came in. One by one we laid them with the multitude of their fathers, seafaring generations, in the windswept graveyard beyond the house. And from each burial Father Patrick came home bowed as though under another load of care. Grief weakened him no less than the endless toil. I would have given all I had to take him away from it, to the South.

It was on the evening we buried Dermot that the sickness came. I found him huddled in the chair in his parlour, unable to speak or move. His old housekeeper and I helped him upstairs and put him to bed and carried the red sods up to his room.

The doctor had to ride out to us over Brandon Mountain. It was that dreaded scourge of the poor, typhoid; a desperate attack. Every day for a week he came, and he and Brigid and I were fighting avenging nature for that dear life. On the last day of October he told me there was no more hope and that I should send for the priest. I went down the village street with him, looking for a boy to ride out with the message; the men were at the street corners, the women at their doors, waiting, dumbly, for the doctor's word. "Pray for him; pray for him!" was all he said. I heard men sobbing as they turned away.

Late in the evening the young priest came and gave the Viaticum to my dying friend. When he had gone and I went in to Father Patrick I found him lying very quiet with a happy radiance on his face. He held out his hand for mine. "Stay by me tonight, Andreas," he whispered. "'Twould be good to have you near when I set out."

You can imagine I felt desolate enough. For months this man had made the whole kindness of my world; I knew I'd never see his like again. And I had no resource. Bitterly I envied the good Catholic people with their boundless faith in prayer. They were praying for him that night, I knew well, in every cottage, and invoking prayers more powerful than their own – All Saints' – all Souls.

When I drew the curtains and lit the lamp at nightfall he asked was it Samhain night. "It is," I answered, and he sighed distressfully: "I ought to be praying for the dead."

There was a little oratory behind the bedroom where he used sometimes to say Mass. "Would you light the altar candles for me, Andreas?" he said. "That way they'll know I didn't forget . . ."

I lit a candle and walking down the draughty passage, opened the oratory door. It was a bare little room with no adornment; there were only a few benches and the altar with its Tabernacle, four brass candlesticks and white cloth, but it was full, to my imagination, of rest. I lit the candles and then, surrendering to a sudden whim, it may be of faith, I prayed. I suppose it was a pagan sort of prayer.

When I went back to Father Patrick his eyes were closed and his breathing was so faint that I thought he had died, until I saw his fingers move feebly along his rosary beads.

There was nothing that I could do but sit in the old chair by the fire putting fresh sods on from time to time, giving him a drink when I saw that he was awake. About midnight he began moaning; his face had grown grey and wan, and his fingers were groping about the quilt. I could see that he was in high fever. "What will they do at all?" he kept murmuring unhappily, and "I ought to be praying for the dead . . ." Then: "Pray that I'll be spared to them awhile, Andreas;"

and again, moaning: "God pity him, he can't pray!"

I knew that he could scarcely live till dawn.

Then the trance-like silence fell again, broken only by the long, wailing gusts of a wind that seemed to blow out of infinity and into infinity again, like a human soul.

We forget, thank God, those intensities of desolation. I only know that the sense of Eternity, always appalling, fell on me in that quiet room – and to me, Eternity was a void. The weak, insane moment in which I had prayed was over . . . the bright flame that had been my friend's spirit was going out . . . after life there was only the Abyss . . . and I could not hold him back; I knew no way . . .

It was an hour or two after midnight, I suppose, when I roused myself and drank some black coffee and went over to my patient to see whether he slept.

He was awake; his eyes were open; he was listening – listening to something which I did not hear. He did not look up at me or speak or move.

I stood, wondering, beside the bed, and presently a sound came to my ears – faintly – a low, rhythmic murmur, like a multitude of voices at prayer. I listened and gradually I heard clearly, much more clearly – a soothing and entrancing sound. It came from the room behind the bedroom – the oratory. I leaned, listening, against the wall. It was prayer; I heard the prayers and responses – but not in Latin – it was

Irish – I knew the soft, rich sounds.

I suppose the language was my only passion – maybe I loved it better, even, than my friend; anyhow, in the mere joy and wonder of hearing it I became oblivious of everything else. Soon every syllable came to me, full and clear; I heard a long unfamiliar litany, full of noble phrases and ancient names – "Naov Finghin . . . Naov Breandan . . . Naov Colmcille . . ." and, after the litany, prayers, long and ceremonious – the whole Mass.

While it lasted I stood spellbound, but when silence came I felt shaken with awful fear; I knelt down, suddenly, by the bed and stared at Father Patrick's face. His eyes were wide open; his lips were moving in quiet prayer; the flush of fever had gone; he seemed to have forgotten me; he said "Amen!"

From the oratory too, I heard a long "Amen," like a contented sigh. I heard the sound of people rising from their knees, and their footsteps, soft and light, as of an innumerable multitude, went past the door. I heard them after a moment on the gravel outside, and low voices began caoining mournfully until a man's voice called quietly, "Na bi ag caoineadh anois" – "Do not be caoining now!" That voice was strangely familiar; caught by it, as one's whole being may be caught by intolerable agony or joy, I waited, in a kind of rigour, for it to come again. I heard it, then – calling my own name, strongly and insistently, three times.

I would have risen; I would have opened the door and rushed out, but Father Patrick's arm was around me, his hand pressed over my mouth. "Don't answer," he whispered urgently, and held me until the noises had passed away.

He lay back on his pillow then, and smiled at me happily, and fell asleep."

FitzGerald, too, smiled happily as he ended his tale. He was tired. Doctor Christiansen's blue eyes were alight. "It was poor Dermot," he asked gently – "He who called?"

FitzGerald answered, "It was his voice."

"He would have loved to take you, instead of that other? If you had answered – is it not so – you would have followed within a year?"

"So Father Patrick said."

"And he recovered – your good friend?"

"Thank God," FitzGerald answered, "he is living still."

Doctor Christiansen spoke wonderingly, "They prayed for him well, those Dead."

HUGH WALPOLE

Hugh Seymour Walpole was born in Auckland, New Zealand in 1884. He was educated at a series of boarding schools in England, followed by Emmanuel College, Cambridge. Walpole's father hoped he would follow him into the clergy, but after three years as a missionary, in 1909, Walpole resolved to become a man of letters. His first commercial success came in 1911 with the novel *Mr Perrin and Mr. Traill*, after which Walpole made the acquaintance of writers such as Henry James and Joseph Conrad, and declared his ambition to become the greatest writer of his era. For the rest of his life, Walpole wrote prolifically. During the twenties he produced more than a novel a year, with *The Cathedral* (1922) and *Wintersmoon* (1928) proving to be great successes. In 1930, he began his most popular series of novels with the historical romance *Rogue Herries*, following it with *Judith Paris* (1931), *The Fortress* (1932) and *Vanessa* (1933). Eventually, he amassed an oeuvre of 36 novels, five volumes of short stories, two plays and three volumes of memoirs. He died in 1941, aged 57. Despite the fact that Walpole sold enormously well on both sides of the Atlantic, and was praised by many of his contemporaries, he is somewhat forgotten now, in part because he was overshadowed by P. G. Wodehouse and others.

A LITTLE GHOST

HUGH WALPOLE

I

Ghosts? I looked across the table at Truscott and had a sudden desire to impress him. Truscott has, before now, invited confidences in just that same way, with his flat impassivity, his air of not caring whether you say anything to him or no, his determined indifference to your drama and your pathos. On this particular evening he had been less impassive. He had himself turned the conversation towards Spiritualism, séances, and all that world of humbug, as he believed it to be, and suddenly I saw, or fancied that I saw, a real invitation in his eyes, something that made me say to myself: "Well, hang it all, I've known Truscott for nearly twenty years; I've never shown him the least little bit of my real self; he thinks me a writing money-machine, with no thought in the world beside my brazen serial stories and the yacht that I purchased out of them."

So I told him this story, and I will do him the justice to say that he listened to every word of it most attentively, although it was far into the evening before I had finished. He didn't seem impatient with all the little details that I gave. Of course, in a ghost story, details are more important than anything else. But was it a ghost story? Was it a story at all? Was it true even in its material background? Now, as I try to tell it again, I can't be sure. Truscott is the only other person who has ever heard it, and at the end of it he made no comment whatever.

It happened long ago, long before the War, when I had been married for about five years, and was an exceedingly prosperous journalist, with a nice little house and two children, in Wimbledon.

I lost suddenly my greatest friend. That may mean little or much as friendship is commonly held, but I believe that most Britishers, most Americans, most Scandinavians, know before they die one friendship at least that changes their whole life experience by its depth and colour. Very few Frenchmen, Italians or Spaniards, very few Southern people at all, understand these things.

The curious part of it in my particular case was that I had known this friend only four or five years before his death, that I had made many friendships both before and since that have endured over much longer periods, and yet this particular friendship had a quality of intensity and happiness that I have never found elsewhere.

Another curious thing was that I met Bond only a few months before my marriage, when I was deeply in love with my wife, and so intensely preoccupied with my engagement that I could think of nothing else. I met Bond quite casually at someone's house. He was a large-boned, broad-shouldered, slow-smiling man with close-cropped hair turning slightly grey, and our meeting was casual; the ripening of our friendship was casual; indeed, the whole affair may be said to have been casual to the very last. It was, in fact, my wife who said to me one day, when we had been married about a year or so: "Why, I believe you care more for Charlie Bond than for anyone else in the world." She said it in that sudden, disconcerting, perceptive way that some women have. I was entirely astonished. Of course I laughed at the idea. I saw Bond frequently. He often came to the house. My wife, wiser than many wives, encouraged all my friendships, and she herself liked Charlie immensely. I don't suppose that anyone disliked him. Some men were jealous of him; some men, the merest acquaintances, called him conceited; women were sometimes irritated by him because so clearly he could get on very easily without them; but he had, I think, no real enemy.

How could he have had? His good nature, his freedom from all jealousy, his naturalness, his sense of fun, the absence of all pettiness, his common sense, his manliness, and at the same time his broad-minded intelligence, all these things made him a most charming personality. I don't know that he shone very much in ordinary society. He was very quiet and his wit and humour came out best with his intimates.

I was the showy one, and he always played up to me, and I think I patronized him a little and thought deep down in my subconscious self that it was lucky for him to have such a brilliant friend, but he never gave a sign of resentment. I believe now that he knew me, with all my faults and vanities and absurdities, far better than anyone else, even my wife, did, and that is one of the reasons, to the day of my death, why I shall always miss him so desperately.

However, it was not until his death that I realized how close we had been. One November day he came back to his flat, wet and chilled, didn't change his clothes, caught a cold, which developed into pneumonia, and after three days was dead. It happened that that week I was in Paris, and I returned to be told on the doorstep by my wife of what had occurred. At first I refused to believe it. When I had seen him a week before he had been in splendid health; with his tanned, rather rough and clumsy face, his clear eyes, no fat about him anywhere, he had looked as though he would live to a thousand, and then when I realized that it was indeed true I did not during the first week or two grasp my loss.

I missed him, of course; was vaguely unhappy and

discontented; railed against life, wondering why it was always the best people who were taken and the others left; but I was not actually aware that for the rest of my days things would be different, and that that day of my return from Paris was a crisis in my human experience. Suddenly one morning, walking down Fleet Street, I had a flashing, almost blinding, need of Bond that was like a revelation. From that moment I knew no peace. Everyone seemed to me dull, profitless and empty. Even my wife was a long way away from me, and my children, whom I dearly loved, counted nothing to me at all. I didn't, after that, know what was the matter with me. I lost my appetite, I couldn't sleep, I was grumpy and nervous. I didn't myself connect it with Bond at all. I thought that I was overworked, and when my wife suggested a holiday, I agreed, got a fortnight's leave from my newspaper, and went down to Glebeshire.

Early December is not a bad time for Glebeshire. It is just then the best spot in the British Isles. I knew a little village beyond St. Mary's Moor, that I had not seen for ten years, but always remembered with romantic gratitude, and I felt that that was the place for me now.

I changed trains at Polchester and found myself at last in a little jingle driving out to sea. The air, the wide open moor, the smell of the sea delighted me, and when I reached my little village, with its sandy cove and the boats drawn up in two rows in front of a high rocky cave, and when I ate my eggs and bacon in the little parlour of the inn overlooking the sea, I felt happier than I had done for weeks past; but my happiness did not last long. Night after night I could not sleep. I began to feel acute loneliness and knew at last in full truth that it was my friend whom I was missing, and that it was not solitude I needed, but his company. Easy enough to talk about having his company, but I only truly knew, down here in this little village, sitting on the edge of the green cliff, looking over into limitless sea, that I was indeed never to have his company again. There followed after that a wild, impatient regret that I had not made more of my time with him. I saw myself, in a sudden vision, as I had really been with him, patronizing, indulgent, a little contemptuous of his good-natured ideas. Had I only a week with him now, how eagerly I would show him that I was the fool and not he, that I was the lucky one every time!

One connects with one's own grief the place where one feels it, and before many days had passed I had grown to loathe the little village, to dread, beyond words, the long, soughing groan of the sea as it drew back down the slanting beach, the melancholy wail of the seagull, the chattering women under my little window. I couldn't stand it. I ought to go back to London, and yet from that, too, I shrank. Memories of Bond lingered there as they did in no other place, and it was hardly fair to my wife and family to give them the company of the dreary, discontented man that I just then was.

And then, just in the way that such things always happen, I found on my breakfast-table one fine morning a forwarded letter. It was from a certain Mrs. Baldwin, and, to my surprise, I saw that it came from Glebeshire, but from the top of the county and not its southern end.

John Baldwin was a Stock Exchange friend of my brother's, a rough diamond, but kindly and generous, and not, I believed, very well off. Mrs. Baldwin I had always liked, and I think she always liked me. We had not met for some little time and I had no idea what had happened to them. Now in her letter she told me that they had taken an old eighteenth-century house on the north coast of Glebeshire, not very far from Drymouth, that they were enjoying it very much indeed, that Jack was fitter than he had been for years, and that they would be delighted, were I ever in that part of the country, to have me as their guest. This suddenly seemed to me the very thing. The Baldwins had never known Charlie Bond, and they would have, therefore, for me no association with his memory. They were jolly, noisy people, with a jolly, noisy family, and Jack Baldwin's personality was so robust that it would surely shake me out of my gloomy mood. I sent a telegram at once to Mrs. Baldwin, asking her whether she could have me for a week, and before the day was over I received the warmest of invitations.

Next day I left my little fishing village and experienced one of those strange, crooked, in-and-out little journeys that you must undergo if you are to find your way from one obscure Glebeshire village to another.

About midday, a lovely, cold, blue December midday, I discovered myself in Polchester with an hour to wait for my next train. I went down into the town, climbed the High Street to the magnificent cathedral, stood beneath the famous Arden Gate, looked at the still more famous tomb of the Black Bishop, and it was there, as the sunlight, slanting through the great east window, danced and sparkled about the wonderful blue stone of which that tomb is made, that I had a sudden sense of having been through all this before, of having stood just there in some earlier time, weighed down by some earlier grief, and that nothing that I was experiencing was unexpected. I had a curious sense, too, of comfort and condolence, that horrible grey loneliness that I had felt in the fishing village suddenly fell from me, and for the first time since Bond's death, I was happy. I walked away from the cathedral, down the busy street, and through the dear old market-place, expecting I know not what. All that I knew was that I was intending to go to the Baldwins and that I would be happy there.

The December afternoon fell quickly, and during the last part of my journey I was travelling in a ridiculous little train, through dusk, and the little train went so slowly and so casually that one was always hearing the murmurs of streams beyond one's window, and lakes of grey water suddenly stretched like plates of glass to thick woods, black as ink, against a faint sky. I got out at my little wayside station, shaped like a rabbit-hutch, and found a motor waiting for me. The drive was not long, and suddenly I was outside the old eighteenth-century house and Baldwin's stout butler was conveying me into the hall with that careful, kindly patronage, rather as though I were a box of eggs that might very easily be broken.

It was a spacious hall, with a large open fireplace, in front of which they were all having tea. I say "all" advisedly, because the place seemed to be full of people, grown-ups and children, but mostly children. There were so many of these last that I was not, to the end of my stay, to be able to name most of them individually.

Mrs. Baldwin came forward to greet me, introduced me to one or two people, sat me down and gave me my tea, told me that I wasn't looking at all well, and needed feeding up, and explained that Jack was out shooting something, but would soon be back.

My entrance had made a brief lull, but immediately

everyone recovered and the noise was terrific. There is a lot to be said for the freedom of the modern child. There is a lot to be said against it, too. I soon found that in this party, at any rate, the elders were completely disregarded and of no account. Children rushed about the hall, knocked one another down, shouted and screamed, fell over grown-ups as though they were pieces of furniture, and paid no attention at all to the mild "Now children" of a plain, elderly lady who was, I supposed, a governess. I fancy that I was tired with my criss-cross journey, and I soon found a chance to ask Mrs, Baldwin if I could go up to my room. She said: "I expect you find these children noisy. Poor little things. They must have their fun. Jack always says that one can only be young once, and I do so agree with him."

I wasn't myself feeling very young that evening (I was really about nine hundred years old), so that I agreed with her and eagerly left youth to its own appropriate pleasures. Mrs. Baldwin took me up the fine broad staircase. She was a stout, short woman, dressed in bright colours, with what is known, I believe, as an infectious laugh. Tonight, although I was fond of her, and knew very well her good, generous heart, she irritated me, and for some reason that I could not quite define. Perhaps I felt at once that she was out of place there and that the house resented her, but in all this account, I am puzzled by the question as to whether I imagine now, on looking back, all sorts of feelings that were not really there at all, but come to me now because I know of what happened afterwards. But I am so anxious to tell the truth, the whole truth, and nothing but the truth, and there is nothing in the world so difficult to do as that.

We went through a number of dark passages, up and down little pieces of staircase that seemed to have no beginning, no end, and no reason for their existence, and she left me at last in my bedroom, said that she hoped I would be comfortable, and that Jack would come and see me when he came in, and then paused for a moment, looking at me. "You really don't look well," she said. "You've been overdoing it. You're too conscientious. I always said so. You shall have a real rest here. And the children will see that you're not dull."

Her last two sentences seemed scarcely to go together. I could not tell her about my loss. I realized suddenly, as I had never realized in our older acquaintance, that I should never be able to speak to her about anything that really mattered.

She smiled, laughed and left me. I looked at my room and loved it at once. Broad and low-ceilinged, it contained very little furniture, an old four-poster, charming hangings of some old rose-coloured damask, an old gold mirror, an oak cabinet, some high-backed chairs, and then, for comfort, a large armchair with high elbows, a little quaintly shaped sofa dressed in the same rose colour as the bed, a bright crackling fire, and a grandfather clock. The walls, faded primrose, had no pictures, but on one of them, opposite my bed, was a gay sampler worked in bright colours of crimson and yellow and framed in oak.

I liked it, I loved it, and drew the armchair in front of the fire, nestled down into it, and before I knew, I was fast asleep. How long I slept I don't know, but I suddenly woke with a sense of comfort and well-being which was nothing less than exquisite. I belonged to it, that room, as though I had been in it all my days. I had a curious sense of companionship that was exactly what I had been needing during these last weeks. The house was very still, no voices of children came to me, no sound anywhere, save the sharp crackle of the fire and the friendly ticking of the old clock. Suddenly I thought that there was someone in the room with me, a rustle of something that might have been the fire and yet was not.

I got up and looked about me, half smiling, as though I expected to see a familiar face. There was no-one there, of course, and yet I had just that consciousness of companionship that one has when someone whom one loves very dearly and knows very intimately is sitting with one in the same room. I even went to the other side of the four-poster and looked around me, pulled for a moment at the silver-coloured curtains, and of course saw no-one. Then the door suddenly opened and Jack Baldwin came in, and

I remember having a curious feeling of irritation as though I had been interrupted. His large, breezy, knickerbockered figure filled the room. "Hullo!" he said, "delighted to see you. Bit of luck your being down this way. Have you got everything you want?"

II

That was a wonderful old house. I am not going to attempt to describe it, although I have stayed there quite recently. Yes, I stayed there on many occasions since that first of which I am now speaking. It has never been quite the same to me since that first time. You may say, if you like, that the Baldwins fought a battle with it and defeated it. It is certainly now more Baldwin than – well, whatever it was before they rented it. They are not the kind of people to be defeated by atmosphere. Their chief duty in this world, I gather, is to make things Baldwin, and very good for the world too; but when I first went down to them the house was still challenging them. "A wee bit creepy," Mrs. Baldwin confided to me on the second day of my visit. "What exactly do you mean by that?" I asked her. "Ghosts?"

"Oh, there are those, of course," she answered. "There's an underground passage, you know, that runs from here to the sea, and one of the wickedest of the smugglers was killed in it, and his ghost still haunts the celler. At least that's what we were told by our first butler, here; and then, of course, we found that it was the butler, not the smuggler, who was haunting the cellar, and since his departure the smuggler hasn't been visible." She laughed. "All the same, it isn't a comfortable place. I'm going to wake up some of those old rooms. We're going to put in some more windows. And then there are the children," she added.

Yes, there were the children. Surely the noisiest in all the world. They had reverence for nothing. They were the wildest savages, and especially those from nine to thirteen, the cruellest and most uncivilized age for children. There were two little boys, twins I should think, who were nothing less than devils, and regarded their elders with cold, watching eyes, said nothing in protest when scolded, but evolved plots afterwards that fitted precisely the chastiser. To do my host and hostess justice, all the children were not Baldwins, and I fancy that the Baldwin contingent was the quietest.

Nevertheless, from early morning until ten at night, the noise was terrific and you were never sure how early in the morning it would recommence. I don't know that I personally minded the noise very greatly. It took me out of myself and gave me something better to think of, but, in some obscure and unanalysed way, I felt that the house minded it. One knows how the poets have written about old walls and rafters rejoicing in the happy, careless laughter of children. I do not think this house rejoiced at all, and it was queer how consistently I, who am not supposed to be an imaginative person, thought about the house.

But it was not until my third evening that something really happened. I say "happened", but did anything really happen? You shall judge for yourself.

I was sitting in my comfortable armchair in my bedroom, enjoying that delightful half-hour before one dresses for dinner. There was a terrible racket up and down the passages, the children being persuaded, I gathered, to go into the schoolroom and have their supper, when the noise died down and there was nothing but the feathery whisper of the snow – snow had been falling all day – against my window-pane. My thoughts suddenly turned to Bond, directed to him as actually and precipitately as though he had suddenly sprung before me. I did not want to think of him. I had been fighting his memory these last days, because I had thought that the wisest thing to do, but now he was too much for me.

I luxuriated in my memories of him, turning over and over all sorts of times that we had had together, seeing his smile, watching his mouth that turned up at the corners when he was amused, and wondering finally why he should obsess me the way that he did, when I had lost so many other friends for whom I had thought I cared much more, who, nevertheless, never bothered my memory at all. I sighed, and it seemed to me that my sigh was very gently repeated behind me. I turned sharply round. The curtains had not been drawn. You know the strange, milky pallor that reflected snow throws over objects, and although three lighted candles shone in the room, moon-white shadows seemed to hang over the bed and across the floor. Of course there was no-one there, and yet I stared and stared about me as though I were convinced that I was not alone. And then I looked especially at one part of the room, a distant corner beyond the four-poster, and it seemed to me that someone was there. And yet no-one was there. But whether it was that my mind had been distracted, or that the beauty of the old snow-lit room enchanted me, I don't know, but my thoughts of my friend were happy and reassured. I had not lost him, I seemed to say to myself. Indeed, at that special moment he seemed to be closer to me than he had been while he was alive.

From that evening a curious thing occurred. I only seemed to be close to my friend when I was in my own room – and I felt more than that. When my door was closed and I was sitting in my armchair, I fancied that our new companionship was not only Bond's, but was something more as well. I would wake in the middle of the night or in the early morning and feel quite sure that I was not alone; so sure that I did not even want to investigate it further, but just took the companionship for granted and was happy.

Outside that room, however, I felt increasing discomfort. I hated the way in which the house was treated. A quite unreasonable anger rose within me as I heard the Baldwins discussing the improvements that they were going to make, and yet they were so kind to me, and so patently unaware of doing anything that would not generally be commended, that it was quite impossible for me to show my anger. Nevertheless, Mrs. Baldwin noticed something. "I am afraid the children are worrying you," she said one morning, half interrogatively. "In a way it will be a rest when they go back to school, but the Christmas holidays is their time, isn't it? I do like to see them happy. Poor little dears."

The poor little dears were at that moment being Red Indians all over the hall.

"No, of course, I like children," I answered her. "The only thing is that they don't – I hope you won't think me foolish – somehow quite fit in with the house."

"Oh, I think it's so good for old places like this," said Mrs. Baldwin briskly, "to be woken up a little. I'm sure if the old people who used to live here came back they'd love to hear all the noise and laughter."

I wasn't so sure myself, but I wouldn't disturb Mrs. Baldwin's contentment for anything.

That evening in my room I was so convinced of companionship that I spoke.

"If there's anyone here," I said aloud, "I'd like them to know that I'm aware of it and am glad of it."

Then, when I caught myself speaking aloud, I was suddenly terrified. Was I really going crazy? Wasn't that the first step towards insanity when you talked to yourself? Nevertheless, a moment later I was reassured. There *was* someone there.

That night I woke, looked at my luminous watch and saw that it was a quarter past three. The room was so dark that I could not even distinguish the posters of my bed, but – there was a very faint glow from the fire, now nearly dead. Opposite my bed there seemed to me to be something white. Not white in the accepted sense of a tall, ghostly figure; but, sitting up and staring, it seemed to me that the shadow was very small, hardly reaching above the edge of the bed.

"Is there anyone there?" I asked. "Because, if there is, do speak to me. I'm not frightened. I know that someone has been here all this last week, and I am glad of it."

Very faintly then, and so faintly that I cannot to this day be sure that I saw anything at all, the figure of a child seemed to me to be visible.

We all know how we have at one time and another fancied that we have seen visions and figures, and then have discovered that it was something in the room, the chance hanging of a coat, the reflection of a glass, a trick of moonlight that has fired our imagination. I was quite prepared for that in this case, but it seemed to me then that as I watched the shadow moved directly in front of the dying fire, and delicate as the leaf of a silver birch, like the trailing rim of some evening cloud, the figure of a child hovered in front of me.

Curiously enough the dress, which seemed to be of some

silver tissue, was clearer than anything else. I did not, in fact, see the face at all, and yet I could swear in the morning that I had seen it, that I knew large, black, wide-open eyes, a little mouth very faintly parted in a timid smile, and that, beyond anything else, I had realized in the expression of that face fear and bewilderment and a longing for some comfort.

III

After that night the affair moved very quickly to its little climax.

I am not a very imaginative man, nor have I any sympathy with the modern craze for spooks and specters. I have never seen, nor fancied that I had seen, anything of a supernatural kind since that visit, but then I have never known since that time such a desperate need of companionship and comfort, and is it not perhaps because we do not want things badly enough in this life that we do not get more of them? However that may be, I was sure on this occasion that I had some companionship that was born of a need greater than mine. I suddenly took the most frantic and unreasonable dislike of the children in that house. It was exactly as though I had discovered somewhere in a deserted part of the building some child who had been left behind by mistake by the last occupants and was terrified by the noisy exuberance and ruthless selfishness of the new family.

For a week I had no more definite manifestation of my little friend, but I was as sure of her presence there in my room as I was of my own clothes and the armchair in which I used to sit.

It was time for me to go back to London, but I could not go. I asked everyone I met as to legends and stories connected with the old house, but I never found anything to do with a little child. I looked forward all day to my hour in my room before dinner, the time when I felt the companionship closest. I sometimes woke in the night and was conscious of its presence, but, as I have said, I never saw anything.

One evening the older children obtained leave to stay up later. It was somebody's birthday. The house seemed to be full of people, and the presence of the children led after dinner to a perfect riot of noise and confusion. We were to play hide-and-seek all over the house. Everybody was to dress up. There was, for that night at least, to be no privacy anywhere. We were all, as Mrs. Baldwin said, to be ten years old again. I hadn't the least desire to be ten years old, but I found myself caught into the game, and had, in sheer self-defence, to run up and down the passages and hide behind doors. The noise was terrific. It grew and grew in volume. People got hysterical. The smaller children jumped out of bed and ran about the passages. Somebody kept blowing a motor-horn. Somebody else turned on the gramophone.

Suddenly I was sick of the whole thing, retreated into my room, lit one candle and locked the door. I had scarcely sat down in my chair when I was aware that my little friend had come. She was standing near to the bed, staring at me, terror in her eyes. I have never seen anyone so frightened. Her little breasts panting beneath her silver gown, her very fair hair falling about her shoulders, her little hands clenched. Just as

I saw her, there were loud knocks on the door, many voices shouting to be admitted, a perfect babel of noise and laughter. The little figure moved, and then – how can I give any idea of it? – I was conscious of having something to protect and comfort. I saw nothing, physically I felt nothing, and yet I was murmuring, "There, there, don't mind. They shan't come in. I'll see that no one touches you. I understand. I understand." For how long I sat like that I don't know. The noises died away, voices murmured at intervals, and then were silent. The house slept. All night I think I stayed there comforting and being comforted.

I fancy now – but how much of it may not be fancy? – that I knew that the child loved the house, had stayed so long as was possible, at last was driven away, and that that was her farewell, not only to me, but all that she most loved in this world and the next.

I do not know – I could swear to nothing. Of what I am sure is that my sense of loss in my friend was removed from that night and never returned. Did I argue with myself that the child companionship included also my friend? Again, I do not know. But of one thing I am now sure, that if love is strong enough, physical death cannot destroy it, and however platitudinous that may sound to others, it is platitudinous no longer when you have discovered it by actual experience for yourself.

That moment in that fire-lit room, when I felt that spiritual heart beating with mine, is and always will be enough for me.

One more thing. Next day I left for London, and my wife was delighted to find me so completely recovered – happier, she said, than I had ever been before.

Two days afterwards, I received a parcel from Mrs. Baldwin. In the note that accompanied it, she said:

I think that you must have left this by mistake behind you. It was found in the small drawer in your dressing-table.

I opened the parcel and discovered an old blue silk handkerchief, wrapped round a long, thin wooden box. The cover of the box lifted very easily, and I saw inside it an old, painted wooden doll, dressed in the period, I should think, of Queen Anne. The dress was very complete, even down to the little shoes, and the little grey mittens on the hands. Inside the silk skirt there was sewn a little tape, and on the tape, in very faded letters, "Ann Trelawney, 1710."

www.ingramcontent.com/pod-product-compliance
Lightning Source LLC
Chambersburg PA
CBHW030534020726
47494CB00004B/1357